# ALIEN SPACE NAZIS MUST DIE!

CHUCK MCKENZIE

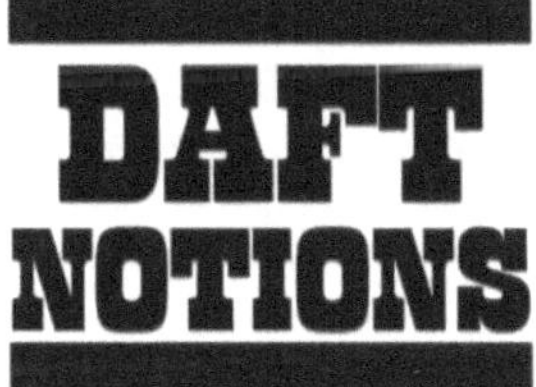

First published by Daft Notions in 2024
Daft Notions www.daftnotions.com
Melbourne, Victoria, Australia
Copyright © Chuck McKenzie

All rights reserved. No part of this book may be reproduced or transmitted in any form or by any means, including Internet search engines and retailers, electronic or mechanical, photocopying (except under the provisions of the Australian Copyright Act 1968), recording or by any information storage and retrieval system, without prior permission by the publisher.

National Library of Australia Cataloguing-in-Publication data.
Alien Space Nazis Must Die!
ISBN: 978-1-923391-00-0 (paperback)
ISBN: 978-1-923391-01-7 (ebook)

Spelling in this book is standard Australian.

Cover Design, Formatting & Editing © All In The Edit
www.allintheedit.com

Fiction, Science Fiction, Humour

This novella is expanded from a novelette of the same title originally published in Elsewhere (CSFG Publishing, 2003).

"For evil to flourish,
it only requires good men to do nothing."

**Simon Wiesenthal**

He blinked, and found himself once again sitting in the shuttle cockpit. He jumped to his feet, then swayed as a wave of faintness and nausea swept over him. His guts heaved, but—

*I don't even have a stomach...*

And suddenly the full weight of reality crashed in upon him. He fell to the deck and lay there, convulsing. Dimly, he heard Kroll say: "So sorry. But better this way…"

Hidden inside the ventilation duct, Lars Janssen peered cautiously through the grille at the shuttle-bay beyond; or, more accurately, at the back of the trooper's head currently blocking his view of the shuttle-bay. The trooper, he noticed, had dandruff; greasy white flakes spilling out from beneath the Nazi's helmet, speckling the collar of his uniform. Lars shook his head reprovingly, then glanced at his watch. Only ten minutes before the explosives went off. If he wasn't off this KillMoon by then…

Lars pushed gently against the bottom of the grille, which swung silently outwards from the wall. He slid forward slightly to brace the back of his neck against the underside of the raised grille to prevent it from swinging shut again, then slowly reached out with both hands towards the back of the unsuspecting trooper's neck…

…paused…

Then lunged forward, grabbed, and *twisted.*

*Snap!*

Lars slid swiftly from his hiding-spot, catching the body as it fell and gently lowering it to the deck. He spared the dead trooper a brief glance—the reptilian yellow eyes already glazing—and smirked.

*Galactic Master-Race? Not from where I'm standing...*

Lars liberated the pulse-rifle from the trooper's death-grip, hefting it with practiced ease, and scanned the bay cautiously. Darkness and silence. Aside from a couple of shuttles parked nearby, dimly visible in the gloom, the area seemed utterly deserted. Lars moved towards the nearest craft.

He'd taken barely three steps before he heard a sound that stopped him in his tracks: a sudden low hum that escalated quickly into the higher octaves before accelerating to a pitch inaudible to the human ear.

*Hummmmmm...*

It was the sound of a pulse-rifle being primed to fire.

Lars stopped in his tracks, finger tightening against the trigger of his weapon. This was bad, but he was nonetheless confident in his own speedy reflexes, so if he could just work out where the other guy was standing—

*Hummmmmm...*

*Hummmmmm...*

*Humm-Humm-Humm-Hummity-Humm-Humm-de-Humm...*

*Dammit!*

Apparently the other guy was standing all around him.

Abruptly, the lights flicked on to reveal a squad of Nazi troopers surrounding Lars, each aiming his rifle unwaveringly at the agent's head. Lars sighed theatrically and raised his hands in surrender. An officer stepped forward and curtly removed the rifle from Lars' grasp. Lars beamed disarmingly. "So…somebody order a candygram?"

"Flippant as ever, Janssen." The mob parted, and a depressingly familiar figure walked forward through the resulting gap.

"Well, well." Lars nodded. "Reichsführer Hottschtepper. I didn't think I'd be seeing *you* again. Last time we met, you wound up on the receiving end of a napalm enema. You must be using a very effective brand of haemorrhoid cream."

Hottschtepper smiled horribly, grey lips peeling back to display a dentist's nightmare of sharklike teeth. "Did you really think you could infiltrate zis KillMoon undetected?"

"Frankly, yes. Mind if I put my hands down?"

Hottschtepper regarded him coolly. "*Ja*. But keep them vere I can see them."

Lars nodded amiably as he lowered his arms. "Sooo…what happens now?"

Hottschtepper smirked. "Now? *You die!* Squad! Prepare to carry out execution!" He sighed as his troopers snapped into position. "Oh—and those of you standing behind ze prisoner? Will you *please* move around to stand with ze others, in case

Janssen ducks? That's how he got avay last time." He stepped quickly out of the line of fire as the troopers repositioned themselves. "Squad ready? Aim—!"

"Um!" Lars raised his hand. "Mind if I blow my nose first?"

Hottschtepper regarded him incredulously. "Ve are about to *shoot* you! Does it truly matter that you die with a nose full of bogies?"

"Sorry," Lars apologised, "it's just that…oh, I'm going to sneeze! Ah! Ah! *Ahhhh—!*" he cupped a hand over his nose, "*—CHOO!*" Unseen by Lars' captors, the tiny grenade hidden up his right nostril flew out into his palm. Lars made a show of wiping his nose with the back of his hand, using the motion to surreptitiously affix the grenade to the nail of his right index finger.

"Are you quite done?" Hottschtepper enquired, with mock-sweetness.

"Yep, all done, thanks!"

"Are you *quite* sure? Vould you perhaps like me to fetch you a Kleenex?"

Lars waved away the offer. "No, all good, thanks. You're good to go."

Hottschtepper rolled his eyes. "*Wunderbar!* So! Squad ready? Aim—!"

"Say cheese!" Lars shut his eyes tightly and flicked his index finger in the direction of the assembled troopers, the grenade shooting through the air to hit the deck in front of the firing squad, where it exploded in a searing flash of light. The entire squad staggered back, flashblinded. Lars leapt forward and tore a pulse-rifle from the grip of the nearest trooper, immediately thumbing the weapon to auto and strafing the squad with plasma-fire. Within seconds Lars was the last man standing—apart from Hottschtepper, who was stumbling blindly towards the exit. "Oh no you don't!" Lars sprinted after the fleeing Nazi, catching up to him within moments, grabbing his shoulder and spinning him around before delivering a cracking blow to his jaw. "*That's* for all the innocents and agents who've died at your hands!" Lars snarled. "And *this—*" a second blow laid the Nazi out cold, "—is for *me!*"

Pausing only to catch his breath, Lars glanced at his watch. Barely a minute left! He sprinted towards the nearest shuttle, charged up the ramp, scrambled into the cockpit and threw himself into the pilot's chair, hands flickering across the flight console. *Closing the ramp! Priming the drive! Ignition!* With a piercing whine the craft shot forwards, punctured the containment field, and flew out into open space. Lars waited until he judged the shuttle was out of range of the KillMoon's anti-spacecraft batteries, then leaned forward and activated the comm. “Hello, KillMoon switchboard? Priority call for Reichsführer Hottschtepper…”

There was a slight pause. Then: “*Ja?*”

“Hottschtepper?”

“Janssen?? Zere is no escape! In moments ze DeathWaffen will be on your trail! And then…*you will meet your doom!*”

“I’m afraid not, Hottschtepper. You see, I’ve left a little gift for you under your KillMoon’s primary reactor.” Lars regarded his watch. “And you’ve got…ten seconds left in which to thank me!”

“*VHAT??*”

Lars’ expression hardened. “Goodbye, Reichsführer!”

“I vill see you in *HECK*, Janssen! *IN HECK!!*”

The comm went dead as a silent flash briefly lit up the endless night of space.

Lars sighed. Mission accomplished. Time to head back to Central Headquarters, debrief, and prepare for the next assignment. No rest for the heroic. An agent’s job was never done. So long as the Alien Space Nazis remained a threat to Intergalactic freedom, there would always be another operation, another counterstrike, another assassination to undertake.

Sometimes, Lars thought, it seemed like he'd been doing this job forever…

"Greeting?"

Lars blinked, then regarded the comm with a frown. "Hello? Who's that?"

"Greeting?"

"Identify yourself, please."

A clattering gargle emanated from the comm, Lars identifying two distinct voices—if indeed it was speech he was hearing, as opposed to a couple of somebodies or some*things* clearing their throats—that he had the distinct impression were addressing one another rather than himself. After a moment, a voice different to the one that had suggested greeting spoke.

"Am Kroll, Commander of Nine Hundred and Twelfth Spawning of Eighteenth Fleet of Elevated Tertiary Hive of Hoosh of Seventeenth Broodworld of Forty Second Quadrant of Fifteenth Outreach of Generation Ark Fleet of Twelfth Great Diaspora of Year of Golden Fettling of Second Glorious Arthrod Empire!"

"Gosh. *That*…is certainly an impressive address. It must make mailing out Christmas cards very time-consuming."

There was a slight pause, then: "What?"

Lars waved a hand dismissively, despite knowing the gesture would go unseen. "Sorry. Agency humour. We have it drummed into us in basic training."

Another pause. "Er…to whom I speak?" Kroll asked eventually.

"This is Lars Janssen of the Intergalactic Anti Alien Space Nazi Agency. State your business, Commander."

More gargling and clattering.

"I *can* still hear you, you know," Lars interrupted wearily.

There was a distinctly embarrassed pause.

Kroll cleared his (?) throat and addressed Lars again. "Believe yourself to be Lars Janssen of Intergalactic Anti Alien Space Nazi Agency? Fight Alien Space Nazis? Fight to free galaxy?"

Lars glanced around the cockpit, then raised an eyebrow and regarded the comm again. "I mean…that's what it says on my onboarding paperwork, yes."

Kroll made an odd rattling sound. "Apologies. No easy way to tell, but…you *not* Lars Janssen."

"I'm not?"

"Not."

Lars smiled thinly. "*Okaaaaaaay*—so, who am I?"

"Not know. But not Lars Janssen. Not agent of IAASNA. Not fight Alien Space Nazis. Not even sit in shuttle right now, talking to us."

"Riiiiiiiight. So where do *you* think I am right now, then?"

"Body connect to 'Ultra-Immersive Entertainment System.' Program running on system is titled 'Alien Space Nazis Must Die!'."

Lars smiled dismissively. "So you're saying I'm…what? Playing some sort of immersive game?"

"Yes. You play *character* named Lars Janssen. We currently observe your gameplay on monitor."

Lars sighed. "Right. Yeah. Sure. Okay. Listen, Commander Kroll, I don't know what you've been smoking, but—"

"We observe you for two cycles now," Kroll interrupted. "Get feel for game. Very…exaggerated. Unrealistic."

"You think my life is unrealistic? I'm…not quite sure how to take that, frankly."

"Not think your life too convenient?" Kroll pressed. "Prison always have hidden exit? Guard never shoot straight? Escape explosion with only seconds to spare? Is believable? Is even vaguely credible?"

"I mean—"

"No! Is not! Is fantasy world! Not real!"

"Go away, Kroll," Lars snapped. "Stop wasting my time!"

More gargling. Then the first voice, clearly a subordinate of Kroll's, said: "We find memory-suppressant installed in system, which clearly reason you not notice being inside a constructed reality. With Commander's permission, I deactivate this now. Just giving you warning."

"Oh, for Chrissake!" Lars leaned forward to switch off the comm, and—

"Deactivating…"

*Light explodes around him. Above, a grossly swollen sun fills the sky. Below, the soil is ash. Deep underground, the sterile remnants of humanity slumber in a drug-induced stasis, bodies laid out on a seemingly endless number of metal gurneys, while artificial intelligences postulate a means to repopulate the Earth.*

*He dives deeper. Remembering...*

*The A.I.s are set to reawaken their wards when a viable solution to their fertility becomes apparent; meanwhile, in order to prevent psychosis due to sensory deprivation, the sleepers remain wired into state-of-the-art gaming modules, all knowledge of their reality suppressed to further cushion them against the weight of their situation. Thus, gamers may fight at the O.K. Corral or Gallipoli, and actually believe they are there. They can take Neil Armstrong's infamous step, or pilot the Enola*

*Gay over Hiroshima, or step into the personas of a vast range of fictional characters.*

*Deeper...*

*He seems to float above himself, looking down at the senseless, emaciated figure huddled on the gurney, cocooned in a web of cannulas and tubes and wiring, a compact gamelink puncturing the top of his skull. A small metallic tag hanging from just above the puncture point reads:*

**RealPlay Games**

**Alien Space Nazis Must Die!**

**A Lars Janssen Adventure**

*He reaches out to touch the wire, and—*

He blinked, and found himself once again sitting in the shuttle cockpit. He jumped to his feet, then swayed as a wave of faintness and nausea swept over him. His guts heaved, but—

*I don't even have a stomach...*

And suddenly the full weight of reality crashed in upon him. He fell to the deck and lay there, convulsing. Dimly, he heard Kroll say: "So sorry. But better this way..."

Later, glancing around the cockpit, he wondered how he could have thought all this was real. The surfaces were too perfect and angular, the colours too monotonous, the buttons and displays obviously mere pixelated representations. *But of course*, he told himself, *the software altered my perception sufficiently for me to accept it all without—*

"Questions?" Kroll asked, over the comm.

Reg Prescott rubbed his forehead, still feeling groggy. Random recollections of pre-game life kept popping into his head like scum floating to the top of a septic tank; a wholly disorienting and unpleasant experience. And there was something odd about his hands; something he couldn't quite put his finger on. "Dunno. Some of it's coming back. Although…" He glanced at the comm. "Are you guys actually, y'know… *aliens?* Or is that just something the game made up?"

"To you, yes, aliens. Last of Arthrod race."

"Last?"

Kroll sighed. "Millennia ago, fight war. Bioweapons induce genetic decay and sterility. Survivors flee in fleet of generation arks, seek new home. Scientists think Earth habitable, hope humanity sufficiently advanced to reverse our sterility. But solar flare hit before we arrive. Qandho make joke at our expense, yes?"

"Qandho?"

"Our faith. Qandho dictate sanctity of life above all else. For us, essential to both spiritual and physical survival. Arthrod once warrior race, governed by instincts not appropriate in enclosed environment of ark. So sublimate aggression by focus upon Qandho. Is ancient religion, long lapsed, but now considered vital to continued survival, and thus again stringently observed. Will teach you dictates of Qandho, once you sufficiently recovered."

*Great*, Reg thought. *Missionaries from outer space*. "Um…actually, I'm an atheist."

Kroll made a querying sound.

"Not religious. Don't believe in God. Or this…Qandho of yours."

"Blasphemy!" Kroll muttered.

"Look, I didn't mean to offend—"

"No, no, am sorry," Kroll apologised, still sounding pissed. "Spend life in company of faithful, is shock to meet infidel."

"Er, yeah…" Reg decided a change of topic was obviously in order. "Listen, perhaps we *can* solve your sterility problem. After all, if the A.I.s can sort out *our* situation, then…" He frowned. "Although…I guess they're *still* looking for a solution, aren't they? Otherwise they'd have woken us up. I don't s'pose it'll take much longer, though. The boffins said five years at the most."

There was a long, awkward pause.

"Hello?" Reg prompted.

"Er..."

"What?"

"No easy way to say," Kroll said slowly, "but—from information we glean from your systems—after you enter stasis, A.I.s realise cannot reverse sterility or other genetic damage from solar flare, and decide only option to preserve humanity is create androids into which human race-memory downloaded. But A.I.s realise preservation of memory alone not appeal to humanity, so decide to leave you in stasis. A.I.s and androids leave Earth to establish own civilisation elsewhere." He paused. "Stasis run on automatic ever since."

Reg took a moment to digest this. "So...how long have I...I mean, how long have all the survivors been stuck in stasis?"

"You play game now for sixty-three local solar cycles. Lucky we arrive. Otherwise..."

Reg's head swam. "It's not true—it can't be! You're lying!" He looked down at his hands; young and far too perfect. "Game!" he called out. "Change player avatar to reflect external image."

His hands flickered, morphing to display the lines and liver spots of advanced age. Reg moaned softly.

Kroll was right. The A.I.s had failed.

Reg buried his face in his hands, feeling numb. "How many left?" he asked eventually. "Most of the other sleepers were older than me. How many survived?"

"Last count," Kroll's subordinate said hesitantly, "three thousand, six hundred, forty-two."

"WHAT?? But…there were over five million of us!"

The Arthrods remained silent.

"Right. Right. Well," Reg said, far too calmly, "it's not the end of the world. We've still got time to look at new avenues of research. Some of the other surviving sleepers would have gone in as children. Infants, even. Minimal genetic damage. And it's not like we need a viable breeding population—I mean, we can look at cloning, or—"

"So sorry," Kroll muttered.

"Oh, for Chrissake! What??"

"Flare activity increasing, not subsiding. Even your youngest now genetically damaged. And neither your cloning tech nor ours up to working around that."

Reg nodded slowly. So. He was going to die. *Everyone* was going to die. The thought left him feeling oddly detached. Too much to take in, he supposed. After almost a minute of silence, he asked: "So. What happens now?"

"Well, leave game," Kroll said. "Come with us."

Reg frowned. "Why?"

"Sorry?"

"I mean…why? You can't help us. We're dead whatever we do. And we can't help you, either. You were hoping we could solve your problems, remember?"

"Of course." Kroll sounded nonplussed. "Cannot save humanity. But extend remaining life by leaving Earth. Our fleet can accommodate all remaining humans…"

*If you leave Earth, you leave the game…*

An icy finger seemed to penetrate Reg's numbness. If he left the game, he left the comfort and familiarity of a fantasy world where he could *make a difference*, fighting the forces of evil; a place where his life actually meant something, even if it was a game-induced delusion. Reality, on the other hand, was a brutal nightmare offering only a bleak, short, ultimately futile existence before his entire species faded into extinction, lost forever in time and memory.

So…if that awful conclusion was inevitable, why take the hard way out?

“Listen,” Reg said slowly, “I appreciate all you’ve done. I really do. But…I think maybe I’ll just stay here.”

There was a shocked silence.

“What??” Kroll demanded. “Cannot be serious! Life most valuable gift Qandho give! To stay in game, to deny reality and life, is…*blasphemous!*”

Reg blew out his cheeks, glancing listlessly around the cockpit. “Well…” he shrugged apologetically, “that’s my decision.”

“But—be living a *fantasy!*” Kroll squawked.

“I mean…sure. But with the memory-suppressant on, I won’t *know* it’s a fantasy.”

“But—!”

“Look,” Reg interrupted, “I get it, okay? The idea of me pissing away what little life I have left inside a computer-generated game obviously offends you on various levels. But there’s nothing left for me out in the real world. I’m already dying of both old age and genetic disrepair, and any friends and family I had must be long gone by now. And there’s nothing I can contribute that’ll help preserve humanity, even assuming humanity could be saved at all. So…I think I’ll just stay in the game. Once again, thanks for…looking in on us, I guess. But please, just let me re-engage with the game. Leave me here and go."

"But...*IS NOT REAL!!!*"

"It's real enough for me," Reg said softly. "And that's all that really matters."

"But—!"

"Game reset!" Reg commanded.

The cockpit vanished.

"...and deliver us from primal urges. Praise be to Qandho."

"Praise be to Qandho."

"General reports," Kroll said in his native tongue, glancing around the table at his subordinates. "Genetics?"

"Nothing new to report, Commander."

"Medical?"

"Aside from our impending extinction? Absolutely fantastic."

Kroll narrowed every single one of his eyes. "Let's keep things professional, shall we?"

"Apologies, Commander."

"Better. Engineering?"

"All good, Commander."

"Security?"

The chief security officer hesitated a moment. "Unfortunately, Commander, there's growing unrest amongst the crew of all fleet vessels. Cases of assault and public brawling are on the rise." He glanced sideways at the head of the genetics division. "Evidence suggests this is largely due to frustration over the recently announced failure of the latest round of fertility treatments, with over-promising of results by the Genetics Division leading to—"

The geneticist lunged at the security officer, hissing furiously, pincers raised.

"Control yourself!" Kroll snapped.

The geneticist bristled momentarily, then grudgingly bowed his head. "Apologies, Commander."

"Isn't it bad enough that our entire species is dying slowly from genetic collapse," Kroll growled, "without attempting to speed our extinction by indulging our primal urges? *Shrakha!* You should be leading by example, not acting like a bunch of stupid, squabbling hatchlings!" He glared around the table. His subordinates glared back, fighting the urge to physically defend their honour. Kroll nodded, satisfied that protocol had triumphed over instinct. "Going forward, the genetics division needs to run any updates through me before making public announcements. Okay? Right. Now, does anyone have anything further to add? No? In that case, I need suggestions on this wretched human, Reg Prescott. You've all read the briefing about him insisting upon remaining in the game to die rather than face reality, which is completely nuts. So—any ideas?"

"Couldn't we just forcibly disconnect him?" the security officer asked.

Kroll regarded the head of the medical division. "Well?"

The doctor shook his head. "Available information suggests there's danger of major psychological damage if we just yank him out of there. Even the relatively gentle intrusion we previously actioned almost gave him a conniption fit, so forcing him out…" He shrugged. "It seems to be a feature of the game itself, though perhaps not an intended one. The tech's relatively primitive and invasive, so physically disconnecting the player without going through certain protocols could even cause physiological damage. Under normal circumstances the game would judge when the player needed to exit the system—pre-set timing, external emergencies, the need for nutrition, etcetera—but the Earthly A.I.s rewired things so that the player never gets woken up, so to speak, as the A.I.s never intended humanity to ever exit the system again."

Kroll looked to the head of engineering. "Could we override that element of the system?"

"Probably. But as the doctor already mentioned, we're not just dealing with a mechanism here. I couldn't vouch for us being able to avoid damage to the players, even if the disconnection safeguards are deactivated."

The security officer raised a pincer. "The game he's in has multiplayer capacity, doesn't it? But he's playing solo, so doesn't that indicate an abnormal mentality for a human? Maybe the other players are more social, so could we look at contacting other humans instead."

Kroll and the doctor shared a look.

"What?" the security officer asked.

The doctor sighed. "We've taken a cursory look at the other players, and every single one of them is playing solo, so while the games were clearly made to accommodate social behaviours…" He shrugged. "Maybe the genetic crisis triggered a widespread psychological change? Anyway, from what we've observed of other players, Reg Prescott is likely to be as amenable to leaving the game as any other human, so it's probably a better allocation of time and resources to keep working on him than to start from the beginning with other players."

"Isn't there a human scientist we could talk to, at least?" the geneticist asked. "Someone who could better assist with *our* crisis?"

The doctor sighed. "Unfortunately, there's literally nobody any better qualified to assist among the remaining humans than Reg Prescott."

"Oh. Really? And what are *his* qualifications?"

"Something called a Bachelor of Arts in Theatre Studies, and ten years working as an Uber driver."

"What does all that mean?" the geneticist asked.

Kroll explained, and a gloomy silence fell across the table.

"Perhaps…" The doctor hesitated. "Our previous intrusion upon Reg Prescott's gameplay, while upsetting to him, didn't seem to cause any *major* psychological damage, possibly because it was actioned within the game only. We didn't attempt to physically extricate him. Maybe if we keep explaining how foolish he's being by denying reality and wasting his life—"

"He didn't exactly respond well last time."

"Yes, but if we kept at him, and also permanently disconnected the memory-suppressant, he might get so sick of the game that he'd leave of his own volition. And then we could roll the same process out to the rest of the humans."

"Do you think that would work?"

The doctor shrugged again. "I mean, Reg Prescott seems like a thoroughly stubborn bastard, and it's fair to assume it may be a trait common to all members of his species. So it might work, or it might not. But I'd suggest we give it the briefest of trials, and if it doesn't work we drop the whole thing as a bad job, and…you know…"

Kroll eyed the doctor sternly. "And what?"

"Well, you know. Leave."

"And why exactly are you so keen to move on from Earth? The flares won't enter their final phase for almost another year."

The doctor glanced around at his colleagues, who all suddenly developed a deep fascination with the table-top. He coughed nervously. "Commander, if I may speak freely?"

"I wish you would."

"Well, it's just that—and I hope my colleagues here will back me up on this—I think most aboard the fleet would admit that it's always difficult to suppress our primal urges, but that the mission to Earth—bringing with it hope for a possible solution to our issues—provided an alternate focus. A much-needed distraction. In addition to Qandho, of course," he added hurriedly, noting Kroll's expression. "But…we know that mission's over now. And we'll have to announce that to the fleet sooner or later. And once we do…well, we've already heard from my colleague here about what loss of hope does to fleet morale." The doctor nodded towards the security officer. "So the sooner we can retrieve these humans from the game, the sooner we can move on, and the sooner you can formulate and announce a new mission to focus upon. And if we *can't* get the humans to leave the game, I think we should probably—"

Kroll leaned forwards, smiling pleasantly. "Who's the Commander here?"

The doctor bowed his head, pouting. "You, Commander."

"Correct. I'm also, you'll no doubt recall, the appointed Most Holy Mouthpiece of Qandho for this fleet, and the Gospel of Qandho dictates our sacred duty is to preserve life, which the retrieval of these humans from their gaming system achieves."

"I—"

"And obviously," Kroll continued, "that means to suggest any course of action in opposition to those sacred duties would count as—" he glanced around the table, "—anyone? Anyone?—*BLASPHEMY!*" he roared, slamming his pincers down against the table and glaring at the doctor.

Silence.

"So," Kroll continued amiably, "in a nutshell, we leave Earth when *I* say. Understood?"

The doctor glared resentfully back at his commander.

Kroll felt a pang of regret. He and the doctor had been good friends once. But the responsibilities of leadership outweighed the niceties and comforts of personal relationships. "So—we'll follow the path you first suggested: disengage the memory-suppressant, and provide ongoing counselling to Reg Prescott on the necessity of vacating the game. Okay?"

"Yes, Commander." The doctor paused. "I…do have an additional suggestion."

"Yes?"

"We provide the counselling via direct visual communication rather than just the in-game audio previously accessed."

"Visual?" the engineer queried. "You mean, enter the game ourselves?"

The doctor nodded. "Exactly. Thus providing a virtual persona for the humans to relate to."

Kroll glanced at the engineer.

"Can we do that? Adjust the necessary connections to Arthrod physiology?"

"I don't see why not."

Kroll glanced back at the doctor. "And you really feel there's an advantage to doing this?"

"Absolutely. It'll make the counselling more impactful by being more personal. More acceptable. More relaxing."

Hiding behind the lavatory door, Lars was just about to leap out and bushwhack the trooper who was answering the call of nature when something utterly nightmarish materialised in front of him.

"*AAAAAAAAAAAAAAARGH!*" Lars screamed, then paused, looking the monstrosity up and down. "*AAAAAAAAAAAARGH!*" he reiterated.

Three metres tall and mantled in a spiny black exoskeleton, the creature stood upon two powerful legs, while four massive arms terminating in crab-like pincers extended from the shoulders. The head was vaguely bug-like, an unsettling number of oversized boiled-fish eyes peering at Lars—Reg—from above a gaping, fang-filled mouth.

"Not think you react so badly," it said mildly.

Reg swallowed heavily. "Kroll?" He cleared his throat. "You, er…took me by surprise, that's all. What are you doing here? I thought we'd said our goodbyes—oh, crap!"

The trooper, momentarily stunned by the unexpected violation of his privacy, had finally recovered his wits sufficiently to draw his sidearm and start shooting. Kroll bellowed as a barrage of laser-fire tore into his body.

"Reset scene!" Reg snapped, pushing his way out from behind the door. The room flickered. The trooper vanished.

Kroll glanced down as his wounds healed. "Can do anytime during game?"

"Only if you happen to *remember* you're playing a game! Look at that!" Reg said sourly, gesturing around the room. "Look at the crappy definition! It's like watching Community TV! And this!" He held up his aged hands. "I look like I've been in the bloody bath too long! I already know I'm old, I don't need reminding of that, but the game's been ignoring my commands to revert back to my gaming avatar! How come?"

"Safety feature. You in game long time, and still have self-image of you as young man, so if you left game still believing you young you suffer shock when see true self. Normally is short period after game when reality bleed through to game as memory-suppressant shut down, in preparation of leaving, to give time to deal with reality."

Reg scowled. "Yeah, well, I'm *not* leaving, am I? So why aren't the gaming avatar and memory-suppressant still operating?"

"Because we switch off."

Reg gritted his teeth. "And why the hell would you do that?"

"Because," Kroll growled, "*none of this real! You need to leave!*"

"Christ! Why does that bug you so much?" Reg snapped. "I *know* it's just a game, but I *don't care!* It's none of your bloody concern anyway, so will you please just re-install the memory-suppressant and go away?"

"Against dictates of Qandho! You stay, you die!"

"I'm going to die anyway, you idiot!"

"But if return to reality, you get to live real life! Qandho dictate we preserve life, no matter how short! To waste remaining life in game is *blasphemous!*"

"*GET OUT!*" Reg screamed, taking a swing at Kroll. "*GET OUT, YOU SELF-RIGHTEOUS PRICK!*"

Kroll jumped back, instinctively assuming a defensive stance. "I go!" he snarled, fighting down the urge to attack. "But be back! Player Two, disengage!"

The doctor and engineer studiously avoided making eye contact with Kroll as the Commander sat up on the couch, yanking the gamelink from his skull. "*Shrakha!* This damned human needs a kick to the cranium!"

The doctor shrugged. "I mean, we're dealing with an alien psychology, Commander. Perhaps we need to consider taking a different approach, regardless of the commands of Qandho…" He paused, regarding the game display as Lars Janssen dispatched a squad of Nazi troopers with an agency-issue pen-knife.

Kroll coughed pointedly.

The doctor started. "Apologies, Commander. I was, er…the game is really quite interesting. From a psychological point-of-view, I mean."

Kroll eyed the doctor suspiciously. Increasingly, there were times when his subordinates' focus seemed to be slipping, and Kroll already had too much on his plate to worry about such things. Just that morning there had been two deaths amongst the crew due to 'natural causes,' an increasingly-used euphemism for genetic collapse. "Do you have any suggestions? Either of you?"

The engineer shook his head. "I'm just here to facilitate the hook up of the system to Arthrod physiology, Commander."

"Then consider yourself dismissed. And what about you?" Kroll asked the doctor, as the engineer left.

"Well, Commander, I know I suggested having us enter the game to make the counselling process more effective…but what if, instead of reasoning with him, we actually made an effort to *increase* his frustration over the disconnection of the memory-suppressant, thereby pressuring him to quit the game of his own volition?"

An evil grin slowly spread across Kroll's face.

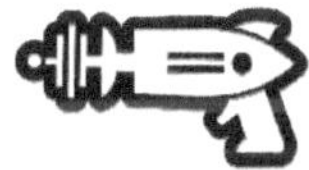

"By ze time we have finished with you," the torturer gloated, "you vill *beg* to die! But first, you vill tell us *everything!*"

Tied to a chair, Lars squirmed in apparent discomfort as he surreptitiously slid the tiny thermal lance from under the callus on his palm. "Had an extra bowl of Sadistic Bastard Flakes this morning, did we?" he croaked, furtively cutting through his bonds. "Well, you'll get nothing from me, Nazi scum!"

The torturer leaned over him, grinning. "Vant to bet?" he hissed, and was extremely surprised when, a moment later, Lars jammed the lance up against his throat, cutting it from ear to ear.

The sentry by the door snapped into action as the torturer fell, swinging his rifle around to cover Lars. Lars froze, knowing he had no chance to move before the sentry pulled the trigger—

*K-chunk!*

Lars smiled pleasantly. "Hi. Rifle jammed?"

"Oh, *scheisse,*" the trooper muttered resignedly.

*Biff! Crack! Snap!*

Lars dusted his hands off. "Sorry to beat and run, but—"

"*BOO!*" a voice yelled in his ear.

Reg shrieked.

Kroll grinned maliciously. "How you even derive pleasure from game? No challenge! Guard's rifle jam at crucial moment? Use knife to kill entire squad armed with guns?"

"They were…really bad shots! Look," Reg snapped, "I'm not leaving, so bugger off! You're interrupting my game!"

"No fun when reminded not real? Hardly worth staying…"

Reg folded his arms across his chest and glared at Kroll. "We both know you can't just shut down the game, which is why you're trying to force me out with this…douchebaggery. But listen, Kroll—I have absolutely no intention of leaving. In fact, I positively look forward to dying in here!"

Kroll's smirk vanished. "*SHRAKHA!*" he screamed, practically foaming at the mouth. "Make mockery of Qandho! I drag you out, no matter how long it take or what others say!"

"What others?" Reg narrowed his eyes. There was a long, awkward pause. "So…someone else is having an issue with your insistence that I leave the game? Who? Your crew? Your officers?"

"Is…*hypothetical* others!" Kroll snapped

"Oh. I *see*." Reg smiled smugly. "So the Commander's having problems with his staff, eh? I shouldn't be surprised, really. Patience obviously isn't a virtue amongst your people, if *your* temper's anything to go by. That makes sense: you're a former warrior race with aggressive instincts probably hardwired, and demonstrably short fuses…" His eyes narrowed again. "Qandho isn't the real problem, is it? I'm going to die whatever I do, and I don't think you're such a religious zealot that you really believe it makes a difference whether I die in here or out there. No, I think what's really got you stressed is that your crew are beginning to get aggressive about the effort you're putting into retrieving me."

Kroll's pincers began to burn. "Not stand here, listen to such *shrakha!*" he snapped. "Player Two, disengage!"

Alone again, Reg leaned back against the wall, pressing his fingers against the cool, smooth tiles. *Not real.*

*Am I wrong to want to stay here? To piss away my remaining existence in a computer-generated fantasy when I could be out there doing something that impacts upon the real world? Something worthwhile, perhaps? Maybe even contributing to solving our sterility issues somehow?*

*No. That's a pipe dream. Even the A.I.s couldn't help us.*

*Nonetheless, a real life. And wouldn't a real life be its own reward?*

He glanced around the computer-generated bathroom.

*But with the memory-suppressant on,* this *could all be as good as real. I could make a real difference* here. *As far as I'd ever know...*

Reg smiled sadly.

"What the frek is going on here?" Kroll snapped, pulling out his gamelink.

"Commander?" The doctor's expression was one of hatchling-like innocence, as the two functionaries standing at his shoulder tried to sidle away unnoticed.

"Don't play dumb with me! This is a restricted area!" Kroll glared at the functionaries. "If I see either of you in here again without permission, I'll have your carapaces steamed! Get out!"

The functionaries scuttled away, bowing and scraping apologetically.

The doctor assumed a defensive stance. "Apologies, Commander. They, er, asked to see the game, and—"

"*Shrakha!* We restricted access to everything pertaining to the humans and their gameplay *specifically* to prevent exposure of the crew to aggressive displays! Do you think I make decisions like this just to amuse myself? I'm trying to stop the crew from killing one another, you idiot!" Kroll's communicator bleeped. "Yes?"

"Security. I'm sorry to report there's been another incident, Commander, with three deaths resulting."

Kroll sighed inwardly, feeling ill. "Another brawl?"

"Yes, Commander."

"Understood. Have a full report to me as soon as possible. Kroll out." Kroll eyed the doctor murderously. "*This* is why we restrict access!"

The doctor shuffled nervously. "Permission to speak frankly, Commander?"

"Go on."

"Look, the crew isn't stupid, Commander. They—*we*—fully recognise the danger of indulging our primal urges, and we're all mostly capable of modifying our behaviour accordingly." The doctor hesitated. "But…"

"What? Get to the point!"

"Well…everyone's already hugely stressed, what with the ongoing health crisis, and the news that the humans don't have any solutions for us. And with the added stress caused by your rigid discipline, and the perception by some that this focus upon dragging the remaining humans out of their gaming systems is a waste of time that's only delaying us from leaving Earth, well…maybe, I don't know…maybe it'd be an idea to…ease off?"

Kroll felt a cold rage bubbling up inside him. His claws burned. "Get. Out," he hissed quietly, desperately fighting the urge to tear the doctor apart.

Growling nervously, the doctor backed out of the room.

*I can barely control my own urges!* Kroll chastised himself. *How can I expect better from my people?* The faces of long-dead friends and family flitted before his mind's eye. Genetic diseases.

Violence. *Not me! Not my people! We* will *overcome these trials, save our species, rescue the humans! Qandho will shine a light upon the way!*

*We cannot give up hope...*

Trembling with fear and shame and anger, Kroll turned, his attention wandering to the game display. Lars Janssen was desperately attempting to steer a burning Nazi cargo ship from what seemed to be inevitable impact with a rapidly approaching wharf, panicking figures fleeing the dock as the vessel careened forwards through churning waves. Three seconds to impact! Two! One!

"Commander?"

Kroll started as the security officer strode into the room. "Yes?" he snapped.

"I've submitted my report to your comms, Commander. I thought perhaps we could discuss it in person. At your convenience, of course," the officer added, glancing pointedly at the game display.

"I've...not had a chance to look at it yet, but we can discuss the essentials right now." Kroll took a moment to collect himself. "So. What are you doing to prevent further violence amongst the crew? Specifically, I mean?"

The security officer hesitated. "Well…obviously that's one of the things I wanted to discuss with you, Commander. Current measures aren't proving as effective as they once were, so—"

"So impose new measures!"

"Commander?"

"It's a simple enough directive, isn't it? Use your initiative!"

The security officer hesitated again. "With respect, Commander, your recent leadership hasn't allowed much room for…*initiative*. You've been tightening your control over pretty much all aspects of fleet operation, instead of allowing your staff to do their jobs. And we *do* know how to do our jobs, Commander."

"Insolence!" Kroll hissed.

"I'm merely stating facts, Commander." The officer shifted subtly in a way that, Kroll realised, would better allow him to defend himself should his commander decide to attack.

"So. You've decided to use my directives as an excuse to, what? Do nothing?"

"Qandho forbid, Commander." The officer glanced again at the gaming display. "And again with respect, I think perhaps that's part of the problem."

Kroll seethed, inching forward as he prepared to—

*What the frek am I doing??*

Kroll abruptly turned his back on the security officer. "You're dismissed. I shall expect a more satisfactory plan of action from you at the next division heads meeting tomorrow. Now go!"

There was a long pause.

Kroll turned back to glare at the security officer. "Yes?" he asked coldly.

"I've been asked to pass on a message to you, Commander. From the bulk of the crew, and all of the division heads and officers."

Kroll braced himself. "Well?"

"It's a formal request for you to authorise departure of the fleet from Earth, Commander. Immediately."

"Indeed. Or what?"

The security officer's tone was neutral. "I can only speak for those already proposing action, Commander, either publicly or in discussion with myself. But I feel a decent summation is that failure to comply with the aforementioned request will further undermine the ability of your people to repress their instinctive aggression. That said, at your behest, everyone has been looking to the directives of Qandho as a means of sublimating our natural urges, but…" he shrugged, "speaking frankly—and yet again, with respect—it's not going to be enough to prevent what might happen next."

"You're speaking blasphemy!" Kroll whispered, now so angry that he was actually smiling. "Qandho dictates that we stay to retrieve the humans—so we do not leave until that goal is achieved. Now...*go and make that directive understood to all.* Do you understand?" His tone brooked no further opposition.

The two angry crustaceans eyeballed each other, an activity for which both were amply equipped. Eventually the security officer bowed his head. "Understood, Commander."

"Now get out of my sight!"

Kroll's claws continued to quiver long after the security officer had departed.

The creature standing on the far side of the combat pit was big, ugly, and had more sets of claws, teeth and spines than the entire menagerie of a masochists' petting zoo. Lars had never seen one before, but there was a vivid description of this particular beastie in the IAASNA Handbook under 'Things To Avoid': a Venusian Shanghorn.

"And me without a perigosto stick," Lars muttered. He tensed, ready to move. Shanghorns were fast, powerful, aggressive, and—worst of all—smart enough to recognise their position at the top of the food-chain, which meant they gave not a single crap about niceties such as caution or restraint when hunting down their prey, which included everything.

Without warning, the Shanghorn pounced. Lars took off around the perimeter of the pit with the beast in hot pursuit. His mind raced. According to the handbook, Shanghorns had only one weakness; a major nerve centre located between the eyes, a blow to which would induce instant paralysis. A perigosto stick would have been ideally suited to the task of hitting that nerve centre. But Lars didn't have a perigosto stick. He didn't even have a pea-shooter. He glanced around desperately. Was there *anything* in the pit he could use as a weapon?

Nothing but hot sand, burning under his feet—

*Hot sand? Heat? Perspiration?*

Lars glanced down at his sweat-soaked trousers, and an idea came to him. Grabbing his waistband with both hands as he ran, he gave a mighty tug, tearing his trousers off. Gripping one of the leg cuffs, Lars rotated his wrist in a lassoing gesture, twisting the sodden pants into a heavy, rope-like length. He glanced back. The Shanghorn was almost upon him. Giving the trouser-rope one last twist, Lars skidded to a halt and spun around to face his pursuer. As the beast flew at him, Lars drew his hand back then snapped it upwards, flicking the end of the rope directly between the Shanghorn's eyes.

*Thwack!*

There was a pause. Then, with a moan, the Shanghorn toppled over and crashed to the ground.

The universe flickered.

"*LEAVE GAME!*" Kroll roared. "Not ask again! Not let you die! Not fail in my duty!"

Reg rubbed his brow wearily. "Look, for the last time—*I am not leaving*, so *PISS OFF!*"

"Cannot do! Qandho not allow! Why you not understand??"

"Qandho, Qandho, Qandho!" Reg sneered. "Stop hiding behind your faith, Kroll! The only thing stopping you from leaving me here is *you!* You can't get the Earthling to bend to your will, but you're too proud to admit defeat! Too proud to let your subordinates see you fail, even though they don't actually care if you succeed! In the end, the only thing that matters to you is that you're in the right! And do you know what else? Deep down, I don't think you actually give a single crap about Qandho!"

Kroll gasped. "You take back!"

"You're just using your religion as a means to justify your actions! And that makes you a bad person!"

"*SILENCE!*"

Reg grinned savagely. "You heard me! You're a bad person, and you should feel bad!"

Kroll hissed furiously. "I tear you apart!"

"Go on, then!"

Kroll trembled, torn between instinct and religious directive. "Qandho not permit!"

"Yeah?" Reg raised his voice. "Acquire razor-tipped staff!" Without giving Kroll a chance to react, Reg lashed out with the weapon that had suddenly appeared in his hand.

Kroll screamed as a pincer-tip fell to the sand, jetting black goo. Hormones surged. Reason gave way to primal rage. Shrieking maniacally, he attacked.

Standing his ground, Reg thrust the tip of his weapon forward, driving the blade deep into Kroll's guts. Kroll bellowed and slammed a pincer down on the staff. Reg staggered back against the wall of the pit clutching a handful of kindling, while Kroll tore the blade from his bleeding stomach. Tossing it aside, he drove a pincer into the wall either side of Reg, caging him. Reg sprang up into the air, executed a perfect summersault, and landed squarely on Kroll's back. Kroll reared up, turning towards the centre of the pit, then bucked forwards. Before Reg could jump free, the buck became a roll, and Kroll tumbled head-first across the floor of the pit, crushing his human opponent into the sand with all the weight and destructive power of a charging rhino.

*Crunch!*

Kroll sprang to his feet, spun around, and began to slam his pincers down repeatedly upon the broken form lying on the ground, crushing bones to jelly and bursting organs, splattering gore across the sand. After almost a minute the bloodlust began to fade and Kroll stepped back, panting as his muscles relaxed. Slowly his mind began to clear…

*What have I done?*

There was a long, long silence.

Eventually, the universe flickered. The shattered corpse vanished, and Reg—whole again—appeared standing beside Kroll,

"Why you force me to do this?" Kroll asked dully. "Belief that we could suppress urges the only thing keep us going. If suppress instincts, perhaps can suppress genetic decay. But now…" He sighed. "When word spread of what I do, dictates of Qandho will be…worthless. Without faith, aggression increase." He shook his head hopelessly. "You doom us all. *I* doom us all."

"Felt good, though, didn't it?" Reg lowered himself into a seated position on the sand. "The thrill of combat, of naked aggression. Can't be healthy, fighting those primal urges. You're an angry species, Kroll. The instinct to fight is probably nature's way of allowing you to let off steam so you don't go completely psychotic."

Kroll bowed his head. "And now nature condemn us. Sterility inevitably kill us, but aggression speed extinction." He sat down disconsolately next to Reg. For a few minutes neither of them spoke, both simply gazing up at the huge, pale, computer-generated sun overhead.

Eventually, Reg shrugged regretfully. "*Everything* dies, Kroll. Every*thing* and every*one*. You. Me. Humanity. The Arthrod. We don't get a choice in that. But we can choose how we go out. We can choose to loosen up and enjoy whatever time we have left, or keep going through all the pointless little motions of trying to halt the inevitable."

"You give this some thought," Kroll noted.

"Yeah, well, it's hard to not spend time thinking about this whole situation when the memory-suppressant's been disconnected. Even with the distraction of the game." Reg gave Kroll an appraising look. "I do have a suggestion to make."

Kroll glanced at him. "Which is?"

Reg told him.

There was a very long silence.

"But…" Kroll said eventually, then trailed off.

"But what? Can you give me one genuinely good reason why not?"

They continued to sit staring up at the sun while Kroll tried to think of one genuinely good reason why not…

Kroll sat up on the couch, carefully pulling the gamelink from his head. For a moment he said nothing, staring contemplatively into the middle distance.

"Commander?" the doctor prompted eventually.

Kroll turned to look at him. "You were watching, of course?"

"Yes, Commander."

Kroll nodded, then glanced towards the door. "How many others?"

"I, er—"

Kroll waved a claw dismissively. "It's fine. I'm guessing that keeping them out must be like attempting to hold back a cosmic storm with an umbrella. But…I do think that perhaps I need to make an announcement sooner rather than later, given that word is almost certainly already spreading as we speak." He gave the doctor a long, hard look. "Don't you agree?"

The doctor considered his words carefully. "I believe that may be the best course of action, Commander."

Kroll sighed. "I'll schedule a meeting for all division heads and officers immediately, followed by a fleet-wide broadcast once we've agreed upon some basic actions going forward." He paused. "I wonder, though…"

"What, Commander?"

"Well, it's probably more of a question for the head of engineering, but…these human gaming systems…"

"Yes, Commander?"

"Well, I wonder how many players their multiplayer mode can accommodate at any given time?"

Lars sighed as he regarded his surroundings; the inside of the vast bunker, the legion of Nazi troopers aiming their rifles at his head, and the bizarre mechanical object standing in front of him. The thing was roughly the size and shape of a watermelon, with four spider-like legs projecting from the lower hemisphere. The upper half was a clear, fluid-filled dome in which floated a grisly lump of crenulated flesh.

"What's this?" Lars asked. "Bring Your Offal to Work Day?"

"Insolence!" A buzzing voice emanated from the mechanism. "I must remember to remove zat tongue of yours before you die!"

Lars raised an eyebrow. "I don't recognise the voice, but the overacting's familiar. *Hottschtepper?* Is that *you?*"

"*Yessss!*" the mechanism hissed. "You may have destroyed my body when you blew up my KillMoon, Janssen…but my brain now controls zis MindenValker!"

"Huh. Glad to see you didn't lose your looks."

"Laugh while you may, Janssen! Zis time, there is no escape!"

Lars shrugged. "If you say so." He paused. "Although…"

"Vhat?" Hottschtepper snapped suspiciously.

"Oh, just that there are two things I should mention before you choke on your own smugness. Firstly, you *really* should get the optics on your MindenValker checked, because you obviously haven't noticed that I'm holding a primed sunflare incendiary device." He slowly held the object aloft. "If I drop this, you can kiss your metal arse goodbye."

Muttering, the troopers drew back.

Hottschtepper fumed incoherently for a moment, then growled: "And ze second thing?"

Lars smiled, then let out a piercing whistle.

Immediately, hundreds of massive, crablike beings began to tear their way into the bunker, ripping effortlessly through reinforced walls, scuttling in every direction as they took up pre-planned positions around the perimeter, where they sat waiting, pincers quivering in anticipation.

The troopers covering Lars immediately lost interest in the agent, pointing their weapons in all directions, unsure of where to aim.

"Assume defensive positions!" Hottschtepper screamed.

The mob of panicking troopers parted as one of the creatures strode towards Lars, regarding the agent amusedly. "Need hand?"

Lars grinned. "Gentlemen, Hottschtepper—may I present Commodore Krotek of the Glorious Arachnoid Empire!"

"*Destroy zem!*" Hottschtepper screamed. "*Destroy zem all!*"

Lars sighed. "You talk too much." He touched a button on the base of the sunflare and the device morphed into something resembling a sonic disrupter, and for the best possible reason. "Part of our new TransMuter range," he explained, taking aim. "Enjoy!"

The disrupter burped softly. Hottschtepper let out a single outraged squawk. Then his brain imploded, spattering the inside of the MindenValker's dome. The mechanism staggered about like a drunken crab for moment, then fell over with a crash and lay still, as dead as its occupant.

A collective moan went up from the assembled Nazi forces.

"Hey!" Lars yelled.

A thousand rifles swung around to cover him. The Arachnoids tensed.

"I've got just one thing to say," Lars continued, then paused for effect before shouting: "*LET'S KICK SOME NAZI ASS!*"

With a roar the Arachnoids swept forward, cutting into the Nazi troopers like Shanghorns into, well, pretty much anything that got in their way. Rifles blazed. Pincers rose and fell. Blood, limbs and internal organs flew in all directions as the troopers screamed and died.

Lars and Krotek stood surveying the chaos for a moment. Then a rifle blast parted the air between them.

"An agent's job is never done!" Lars shouted above the din.

Krotek gestured invitingly. "After you?"

Lars opened his mouth to reply…then hesitated as something tickled the back of his mind; a vague sense of something forgotten. There was a flicker of images. A flaring sun. An old man lying on a bed. He frowned, grasping, trying to remember, but it was like moving through a dark and unfamiliar house, opening one dilapidated door after another, endlessly searching, until—

And then, abruptly, it was gone.

Lars blinked, shaking his head. "Sorry—what?"

"I say," Kroll growled, "is time to join party?"

Lars grinned. "Sure. Why not?" Gripping his disrupter tightly, he took a deep breath. "*ALIEN SPACE NAZIS MUST DIE!*" he yelled joyously, and he and Krotek leapt once more into the fray.

# About the Author

## CHUCK McKENZIE

Chuck McKenzie was born in 1970 and is still not dead. He is an award-nominated author of numerous science fiction and horror stories, and he hopes one day to be described by his neighbours as having seemed like such a nice man. You can stalk him on Instagram at **@chuck.mckenzie.author**

# Also By

## CHUCK McKENZIE

*Worlds Apart* (Novel, Hybrid Publishers 1999)

*AustrAlien Absurdities: Comic Tales of Science-Fiction, Fantasy & Horror by Australian Authors* (Anthology, co-edited with Tansy Rayner-Roberts, Agog! Press 2001)

*Confessions of a Pod Person* (Collection, MirrorDanse Editions 2005)

*Conversations With My Cat* (Collection, co-authored with MacReady McKenzie and Ripley McKenzie, Daft Notions 2023).

*The Dark Man, By Referral and Less Pleasant Tales* (Collection, Daft Notions 2024)

*All I Want For Christmas* (Novella, Daft Notions 2024)

*Daily Grind and Other Astounding Stories of Mundane Matters* (Collection, Daft Notions 2024)

*Time Spent With A Cat* (Novella, Daft Notions 2024)

# Also By

## CHUCK McKENZIE

## CONVERSATIONS WITH MY CAT

What does Schrödinger's Cat have to do with a chewed computer cord? How do you fit work around a cat's napping schedule? Why do cats change their minds as soon as you open the door for them?

These and other conundrums are addressed in this collection of discussions between one man and his cat, wherein are tackled many of the greatest issues of our time: politics, religion, culture, history, human rights, and poop.

You'll laugh, you'll cry, it'll change your life. Or not. Frankly, we'll say anything to get you to buy this book, which is – fair warning – NOT FOR KIDS, as the cat featured herein is a real pottymouth.

# Also By

## CHUCK McKENZIE

## TIME SPENT WITH A CAT

Time Spent With A Cat: the best Hard SF gonzo-fantasy murder-mystery novella featuring a possibly-imaginary talking cat you'll ever read, probably.

My name's Jim Carpenter. I'm a private eye.
And business has been in the toilet since everyone found themselves saddled with an ethereal entity that floats beside them.
Mine is a wiseass talking cat. I hate cats.
But's that's not my biggest problem, because a cashed-up frenemy from my military days has just given me six hours to solve the murder of a scientist who was working on something very special for the Special Weapons Division. Shot in the head, only one possible killer, witnesses on the scene within seconds.

Should be an easy case, right?

Except that, impossibly, the weapon and bullet have both vanished.

And the clock is ticking.

# Also By

## CHUCK McKENZIE

## ALL I WANT FOR CHRISTMAS

++the g'norr are your friends — welcome them — love, serve, obey++

**It's Christmastime, and a full-scale covert alien invasion is underway!**

**Bullied back into service, retired g'norr squadleader Sneet must help claim the primitive planet Earth for the glory of the G'norr Dominion by undertaking a mission that involves brainwashing human children in preparation for the takeover... all while working undercover as a shopping mall Santa.**

**With the might and technology of a galaxy-spanning extraterrestrial empire pitted against a bunch of primitive juvenile primates, nothing could possibly go wrong. Right?**
**Right...?**

# Also By

## CHUCK McKENZIE

## THE DARK MAN, BY REFERRAL

## AND LESS PLEASANT TALES

***STEP INTO THE WORLD OF THE DARK MAN:***

***PLEASE HAVE YOUR REFERRAL READY...***

An abused child encounters the local legendary boogeyman, and finds himself querying the definition of 'monster'...

Two time-travellers observe The Crucifixion, and discover a horror far beyond the brutality of the event itself...

An inhuman predator establishes its feeding ground in a small rural town —but does it have competition...?

In this collection, representing the darker work of author Chuck McKenzie, you'll find tales of zombies, kaiju, and alien invaders; of visits to Hell, and to quiet suburban streets; of Lovecraftian entities and spectral terrors.

And other, far less pleasant tales than these...

# Also By

## CHUCK McKENZIE

## DAILY GRIND

### AND OTHER ASTOUNDING STORIES OF MUNDANE MATTERS

**THE DIFFERENCE BETWEEN THE EVERYDAY AND THE ASTOUNDING DEPENDS ENTIRELY UPON YOUR VIEWPOINT...**

A conversation between two aliens reveals that some aspects of working life are universal, such as job satisfaction—or the lack thereof...

A private detective investigates an impossible murder, unwillingly assisted by an annoyingly talkative cat who may or may not be completely imaginary...

A daring hero defiantly battles Alien Space Nazis for the fate of the galaxy—but doesn't it all seem just little bit...unlikely....?

In this collection, comprising the science fiction stories (including three novellas) of author Chuck McKenzie, you'll find tales of time-travellers, interstellar scam artists, and interdimensional expeditions; of alien invaders masquerading as Santa, and others offering services that sound too good to be true; of bushrangers battling Wellsian Martians, and the unthinkable results of doubling the average human lifespan.

And other astounding stories of relatively mundane matters...

**Publisher of the Niche,**
**the Oddball,**
**the Unsettling...**

Small press publisher operating out of Melbourne, Australia.

Current and forthcoming publications include science fiction and horror titles, management guides, single-author collections, novels and novellas, and funny cat books.

For more information and to purchase our titles go to:

www.daftnotions.com

www.ingramcontent.com/pod-product-compliance
Lightning Source LLC
Chambersburg PA
CBHW031257210726
48287CB00003B/1074